LOGOMACHY

A Short Story Collection

George Saoulidiis

Mythography Studios

A WORD

A battle of words.

This is a collection of my short stories that have to do with language, words and seeing logos in a different way.

Most of my stories have some sort of wordplay, double meaning or innuendo, but these specifically have to do with language.

Being bilingual has allowed me to see the world a little bit differently. I can see the limitations of the English language when compared to Greek, and I can see how language is the source code of our brain that literally shapes the way we think.

This collection came up when I had to submit a short story for a language/translation theme, so I gathered these up from my bibliography and put them all into a separate volume for you to enjoy.

George Saoulidis,
Athens, 2020.

MEAT THE ALIENS

"The Encephalons are a friendly race of aliens," the General said.

"Oh? You've dealt with them?" the computer nerd asked, biting his nails.

"They are talkative, polite and have not threatened us with their superior technology. So, yes, that places them in my 'friends list,' as much as an alien can be considered that."

"Right. And they offered to show us their technology?" the nerd asked, wanting to be anywhere but there.

"They have approved a single person to receive a tour of their spaceship and, well to pop the hood, in a manner of speaking." The General poured some whiskey from his drawer. "I shouldn't be drinking while in the midst of giving orders, even to a specialist such as you, but you'll excuse me under the circumstances."

"Of course, sir. Drink away."

"You need one as well." The General poured one for the specialist as well.

He drank it, the nasty bite down his throat letting him calm down a little. The buzz was almost instantaneous, it was some of the good stuff. "Thank you, sir. Please, continue."

"Since they're letting only one person on board, we considered sending someone that could absorb as much information as possible in the small amount of time he'd be up there."

The specialist opened his mouth, then shut it. Then opened it again. "But why me? Surely an engineer or-"

The General raised his palm. "We've put much thought into it already. An engineer would be unable to see anything about their FTL technology, it's all exotic matter and other crazy things as I've been told. A doctor was our second choice, in case they turn hostile, she might notice some weakness in their physiology while they have their guard down. A weapons specialist would have the same issues as the engineer. That leaves us computers."

The computer specialist gulped. "Of course, sir."

"The objective is to remain friendly and diplomatic. You are to do nothing that would endanger our relations with the alien race. Even if they somehow take you hostage, I'm ordering you to remain calm and surrender peacefully. We will negotiate your release via diplomatic means. You are not to defend yourself unless your very life is on the line. Got it, specialist Barnes?"

"Yes, sir!" the nerd said, snapping at attention and saluting.

"Good. Now report at the helipad on the double!"

Barnes forcibly stopped himself from gulping so much. He was sure he'd strain a neck muscle or swallow something important that wasn't meant to be swallowed.

"Please, follow me," the Encephalon said. He could easily pass off as a human, having no hair, slightly enlarged eyes and big thumbs. But that was what evolution experts said would happen to humans as well, so that didn't really bother Barnes at all. What did bother him was that they were aliens from across the stars, visiting Earth as if it was a tourist destination. He spoke in his language in the communicator in his hand, similar to a cellphone.

Barnes followed. "Um, my name is Barnes."

"I'm Volo, nice to meet you," he said, shaking his hand. He led Barnes up the stairs and into the alien spaceship.

Barnes looked around like an idiot, of course, jaw hanging. Everything looked cool and futuristic, but since it was all made for humanoids, things were exactly how you'd expect. As in door heights, corridor sizes, steps. The ship even followed the same layout as humans, with hatch doors that could isolate parts of the ship in case of a hull breach. "Everything looks familiar, somehow," Barnes smiled.

"How's so?" Volo asked.

"Don't get me wrong, it all looks frickin' cool," he chuckled. "But at the same time, it makes sense. It's not alien to me, you know?"

"Same shit, different solar system," Volo shrugged. The Encephalons had gotten a reputation in the First Contact team about how easily they picked up slang. It was like talking to a mate from England, it only took them like five minutes to get the hang of it.

Barnes laughed. "Exactly! I mean, this could have been an Earth vessel, for all I know."

"I get your point. Your First Contact team has been gracious enough to send us schematics of your non-classified vessels, and we've also seen remarkable similarities."

Barnes felt a lot calmer. Sure, they were alien. Sure, they came from the stars. But they were friendly and in the end, not at all dissimilar to humans. He even liked Volo, no wonder they sent him to do the tour. "We could both help each other if you did the same."

Volo stopped and turned to him.

Barnes thought for a second that he'd blown it.

Volo smiled warmly. "We can do that. Please, follow me," he said again.

Barnes followed, this time with a pep in his step. Were they gonna just show him advanced tech, just like that? He pinched the soft flesh of his hand, making it bleed. He needed the adrenaline, needed to be alert. Observe everything, forget nothing. This could be the only chance the Encephalons would ever give them.

Volo brought him to a clean room, or rather the prep room for cleaning up.

"I recognise this. It's a negative pressure clean room, just like where we make integrated circuits." Barnes looked aroud.

Volo smiled. "Then you are familiar with the procedure. Please, scrub down and put on the suits with me, the mainframe room needs to be absolutely clean of contaminants."

Barnes was now absolutely giddy with excitement. He was

gonna be the first computer guy to lay eyes on their computers. He stripped down to his underwear and put on the suit. Volo did the same, glancing at him to see if he needed any help. Barnes didn't need any, he was an actual computer specialist, having worked a clean room before at DARPA. He put on the part on the head and inspected the seals. Everything was well-made, snapping in place, feeling firm and durable. "I think I'm good to go." As soon as the words left his mouth, he realised that this might be the hostage situation the General warned him about. But, he realised, that he was willing to risk it.

What would it be? A quantum computer, certainly. Nah, humans had already built a crude version of that, and they were nowhere near space-travel at this scale. It must be something even bigger and faster that quantum.

Volo finished suiting up. "With your permission," he said, and when he got an affirmative nod he put his hands around the seals of Barnes' suit. Satisfied, he smiled again. "Follow me, please."

Barnes followed into the clean room.

Volo opened his arms in a presentation and said, "This is the mainframe."

Barnes ran his gaze slowly from bottom to top. His breathing became frantic, his hands trembled. The suit felt like a million degrees, and he wasn't taking enough air through the filter. There were three other Encephalons working around the mainframe, wearing suits like them.

And, in the middle of the room, was a giant brain floating inside a transparent box.

There was an eerie red light, and the brain looked squishy and pink. Barnes could swear he could see the signals firing in the synapses.

"This can't be the mainframe," Barnes wheezed after a long while. He thought his eyesight was getting blurry.

"I assure you, it is," Volo said proudly. "It's the way we calculate spacetime travel. It's impossible to navigate otherwise."

Barnes gulped. Get yourself together, man. This is a unique

opportunity, don't waste it. "O-Okay," he stuttered. "And the computers link up to the brain?"

Volo turned to him, frowning. "What do you mean? That is the computer."

"No, I mean the electronics, the ones in your machines."

Volo kept looking as if he wasn't understanding his words. Which was weird, because they even picked up pop references and slang. "That's what's in our machines, specialist Barnes, I assure you."

Barnes was frustrated now. He stepped closer to Volo pointed at his pocket. "No, your electronics. The integrated circuits. What are they made of?"

Volo brought out his communicator. Every Encephalon had one, it was like carrying a phone around. "This one?"

"Yeah, that. Can you crack that open?"

Volo offered it to him. "Be my guest."

Barnes accepted the phone and spun it around. He found a notch, just like a phone from Earth. It was hard to dig his nails into it with the gloves on but he managed it somehow, and popped the lid open, expecting to see the familiar block of integrated electronics.

What he saw, would haunt him until the end of his days.

The being, was squished, rectangular, thin. It breathed. It hooked up to the screen and the buttons, and in his shock, Barnes pulled the screen apart, making it separate with a disgusting squish.

Barnes looked up at Volo, then at the giant brain in the box. "These are your electronics?"

"Of course," Volo said helpfully. "What else would we use?"

The cellphone's eye blinked and followed Barnes' face straight into his nightmares.

The End.

CHUCKING MOON ROCKS ON THE BACK OF MY PICKUP TRUCK

Wade chucked a rock at the back of his pickup truck. He loved his pickup truck, it was the best one in the entire moon, literally. There was none other in the entire rocky place, no siree.

He loved that truck. He washed it, he took care of it, he drove around in it.

The job wasn't much, but it was an honest day's work, chucking rocks at the back of his truck, driving around to where the computer told him to, stopping, getting out, chucking more rocks.

Even an idiot could do it, but he'd get bored very quickly. Wade was the perfect kind of idiot, he could both do the job and not get bored. No siree, all he needed was his country songs and his beer and his trusty ol' truck.

Songs were easy to obtain, and the computer could even make more up as it went! How cool was that? It claimed they were 'formulaic' or something and Wade just pressed a button and the damned thing spat out more singin' just like that!

Wade was wary at first, but he liked some of the new ones the computer made so he stored them and played them on repeat.

Yeah I'll have Callisto beer
But I don't wanna hear
No songs about moon trucks

No no no
No more songs about moon trucks
No no no no no

He sang along to the tune, bobbing his helmet up and down. He reached out with his rake and picked a small rock. He could use that for the smaller ones, the large ones he had to use a shovel, maybe a pickaxe. It was an honest day's work.

Wade chucked the rock at the back of his truck. It was funny how gravity was light on Callisto, being a small moon and all that, so he could chuck it far with a flick of his wrist. It took him a while to get used to it but he got it eventually, chucking rocks like an NBA VIP. Yessir.

Wade could do with a beer, right about now. He checked his watch and the computer display, he was within the route parameters. He was gonna pick up one more rock, chuck it at the back of his truck and get inside to cycle the airlock, unscrew his suit's helmet, and drink Callisto beer.

He could practically taste it already, that sweet and sour taste that the autobrewery produced. He loved that machine back at the Hub, it was his pride and joy. It made his beer, so he took real good care of it.

Wade absent-mindedly picked up another rock. It slipped from his rake, so he leaned down to grab it with his hand.

He stretched back, and was about to chuck it towards the truck.

"Hey, wait," someone said.

"What in God's name?" Wade started, looking around. He turned off his music, looked around. There was no one there. He shrugged and extended his throwing arm.

"No, don't."

"Aw it cannot be!" Wade said, freezing in place, now spinning around frantically. This time he heard it clear as day. The voice.

"Down here. In your hand."

"Ah!" Wade got startled and dropped the rock. It fell and

rolled a bit on the icy surface of the moon.

"That was rude," the rock said.

"You can speak?" Wade asked, squinting at it. He held his pickaxe up high, ready to strike.

"Obviously."

"Okay. Are you a rock?"

The rock sputtered. "We're not all called rocks, you know... We're... Okay, never mind, yes. I'm a rock."

"Okay. I'm gonna leave you be and go back to my truck," Wade said, stepping away to do just that.

"Wait, what? Aren't you curious about me? I mean, you found alien life on an icy, rocky moon."

Wade shrugged. "Not really. Do you have any beer?"

"No, I don't have any beer. I'm a rock."

"Do you have music? Rock and roll?" Wade snickered.

"Yes, we have music. Wanna hear?" the rock asked.

"Sure. Let me see."

The rock made some crumbling sounds.

"That's it?"

"It's one of the finest ballads of my species," the rock said proudly.

"It ain't no country music, that's for sure."

"Was it the one from before? I liked those vibrations."

"Yeah, wanna hear it again?" Wade lifted his wrist and typed on the keyboard with the other. He started the music, lowering the volume a bit. He bobbed his head to the rhythm.

"I don't wanna hear, no songs about moooon truuuucks," the rock sang. "Yeah, it's nice."

"Glad you appreciate, rock." Wade tipped his head in a cowboy's salute. "Well, I must be off. There's a schedule to keep."

"For what?"

"For rock samples."

"But why are you gathering those rock samples in the first place?"

"Those scientists back home really seem to like 'em."

"And they're looking for what exactly?" the rock asked, as if talking to a child, presenting a string of thought.

"To find alien life or whatever. I dunno."

"But I am alien life," the rock exclaimed, losing its patience. "You've found it."

Wade pushed his chin forward. "Ungh... I dunno man. I'm not sure."

"You're not sure about what? From your perspective, I'm an alien. And I'm talking to you, so I'm intelligent."

"I don't think you are. I mean, no offence, but you're just a rock," Wade said, his palm up to it.

"But-But I'm speaking to you? I'm even sure I have a more extensive vocabulary than you!" the rock sputtered.

"I dunno... Nah, this cannot be." Wade scratched the outside of his helmet, mulling it over.

"Seriously, what is there to think about? Just get me in touch with a scientist," the rock said.

"What would a rock have to say to a scientist?" Wade asked, laughing.

"The very fact I'm able to talk is enough!" the rock said, losing its patience. "Really, man, how thick are you?"

Wade thought about it for a moment. Then he waved the comment away with a gloved hand. "Nah. I'm leaving, my beer is waiting for me in the truck." He started to walk towards his truck.

"No, wait! Wait!" the rock's voice became smaller and smaller as he left it behind him.

Wade climbed on his truck. He stopped, thinking it once again. He hopped back down on the ground, his boots crunching on the frozen rocks below. He reached out and picked one that was about the same size as that goddamn talking rock from earlier on, and he chucked it at the back of his truck.

There, quota met. The computer would be happy.

He climbed on his truck, went inside the familiar cabin, cycled the airlock, unscrewed his suit's helmet, and drank Callisto beer.

"Ah, yeah!" he said, smacking his lips together with the taste of the beer on them.

He sniffed, then held on the steering wheel. The computer was happy about the day's quota and rock samples, so he could just head on home and put his feet up.

One hand on the wheel, a beer in the other, songs in his ears and his face towards the Hub, he felt great about livin'. He'd let nothing disturb that, no siree.

"Stupid rocks and their talkin'," Wade shook his head, driving on home.

The End.

THE KISS OF
THE SPHINX

One layer of skin at a time. The cost of failure didn't sound so bad at first.

I mean, humans have what, seven layers of epidermis or something like that?

He had so many tries to figure out the Sphinx's riddle.

Yeah...

He looked down at his hands, winced from the pain and took off his spacesuit's glove. The hand was... Well, it was sinewy. He flexed the fingers, he could see the muscles on his lower arm pulling against the tendons that controlled the fingers. Well, look at that! There were no muscles inside the hand, only the one for the thumb.

How interesting.

And, ow.

Actually, he didn't hurt at all. That was three tries ago, when he gave the wrong answers and the top layers of his skin got peeled off. After a few tries, there was no pain, only the after-thought of one. He... felt like there should be pain, does that make sense? Like a phantom limb, he had phantom skin.

He was certain his condition could not have been sanitary at all, but he had no choice, really.

It was the Sphinx, or turn back.

And turning back was not an option.

The Sphinx wiggled her lion's toes. She tried to look in-different, but he knew that she enjoyed this ordeal of his.

He popped his lips, or at least tried to. It was surprisingly hard to breathe without lips. It was as if they performed a function, you know?

The Sphinx grinned at him, showing her canines. "Do you want me to repeat the riddle?"

"No," he whined. "I remember it."

He paced up and down the chamber, he was certain it wasn't good for his skin or lack thereof to rub it any further, but it helped him think. "I'm blunt as a rock, dimorphus as light, white as the snow, brittle as the night. What am I?"

He bobbed his head while pacing some more. "What am I, what am I?"

He spun on his heels, pointing at the Sphinx. He opened his mouth, thinking his words carefully. "I am... a supernova! Did I get it? Did I?"

The Sphinx raised her paw and exhaled deeply. The mist from her lungs flew in the air and went straight for him.

"No, no, come on. That was it, I'm sure this time. It can't be wrong." He snapped his visor shut in a futile attempt to save his skin.

The mist went through the minuscule gaps in his spacesuit, plus his open glove connections. There was pain, but it was far less than the other seven or so times before. His nerves must have been flayed off along with the rest.

The Spinx didn't move, she simply said, "Wrong answer."

"Dammit!" he hissed, feeling his tongue weird. Wait, was his tongue just an exposed muscle now? "Ouch, that hurts. Ouch." He hurt at each breath. He hurt while moving around, his exposed skin touching on the insulating layers of his spacesuit. And what was most important, he had gotten the damn riddle wrong again.

Why?

It was obvious. It's brittle, it's bright. Whatever. He was far too distracted to think clearly, he tried to sit down, but it was worse. It seemed that you needed skin to sit on your butt. Imagine that. His gluteus maximus or whatever was pulling on his other things far too tight, it hurt. It probably injured him as well.

He stood up, but didn't pace up and down any longer.

He pulled up the keyboard on his left wrist, decided to use the voice synthesiser, the one they used in case communication was troublesome. His tongue hurt far too much for him to be using it any more. The synthesiser used his own voice, anyway, it was perfectly natural. Although it missed on some particular inflections of speech sometimes.

He typed in, "What did I get wrong this time?" and the voice synth said it out loud.

"I can't answer that. But the answer you gave is wrong, just like the ones before that," the Sphinx replied, repositioning her enormous body into a more comfortable position. She smiled, her human face pulling back to reveal her very sharp teeth.

"What are you doing, are you eating my skin layers?" he asked through the voice synth.

"No. Well, yes," she replied. "In a way."

He squealed something incoherent. He typed furiously, making many mistakes, but the autocorrect had been trained for his usual ones. "You are what now?"

"Yes, alright. I guess I am eating you, little layers every time you fail to answer correctly."

"Oh."

The Sphinx smiled again, this time without showing her teeth. She looked normal, from the midriff up. A bare-breasted woman with plenty of curves and a tiny hint of ginger fur. She moved her lion's tail about, like slapping at flies.

"Can I try again?"

"Of course."

He felt the inside of his mouth, his teeth had begun to hurt, a lot. The roots were becoming exposed, and he kept his mouth shut so it would be moist. That seemed to make it better. His tongue felt weird, as it was numb. And his nose, oh, everything burned every time he inhaled. His nasal cavity hadn't been this clean in his entire life.

Everything ached and prickled and hurt him. And he was definitely going to have some serious infections, even if he somehow got out of this mess.

"Is there some other way you can let me pass?" he asked with the synth.

"I don't see one. This is how you pass the test, answer the riddle."

"Okay, I'm dumb. You got me. Give me another riddle, one for kids or something."

The Sphinx smiled bitterly and shook her head left and right. "I'm sorry, but that's not possible."

He typed a whole lot of expletives and then deleted them, balling his fists and feeling the pain of his palms. After a minute, he calmed down and finally wrote. "Okay. I have another guess."

The Sphinx perked up. "Oh? Please, tell me."

"You never get tired of this riddle thing, do you?"

"I do not."

"Okay, it's ice. The answer to the bloody riddle is ice. Okay? It's everything, blunt, brittle, white, it has a double nature..."

The Sphinx raised her paw again, and exhaled her usual mist.

"Oh, hell no!"

The mist assaulted him and ate up a thin layer of his body. There was no skin left, so he guessed the nanites or whatever she was using started to flay off sinew and muscle. He didn't hurt any more than before, but it couldn't have been good for his overall health.

"Dammit!" he synthed, but the voice did not come out as loud as he wanted to express himself.

"I'm sorry," the Sphinx lowered her head.

He breathed in deep, hurting all the way down to his larynx. "Okay, lemme think. It's not ice. It's not the sun. It's not a black hole. It's not a white hole, and it's not a supernova. It's not a dog, it's not a candle, and it's not a tree."

"And it's not 'Fuck you and your riddles, Sphinxy,' which was your third try," the Sphinx added.

"Yeah..." he glared at her.

She shrugged. "You insisted I count it as a try."

"I did. Silly me." He paced up and down, it hurt something less now. Or the damage was so extensive, it didn't even matter. He thought about the soles of his feet sloshing around in his boots. He also thought about his balls, and he had a weird sensation down there in general, but he didn't want to investigate further. Because if what he feared was true, he'd just find a way to kill himself. He felt a tug on the base of his testicles, a feeling that he hadn't ever felt before. A sort of stringey pull, along with the pain, of course. He shook his head and put it out of his mind.

He turned to the Sphinx. "I have another answer," he synthed.

"Very well. I'm listening."

She did.

This time he thought about it some more. He paced up and down, and he immediately froze. He felt something snap and then sloshing down his pants and into the lining of his calves.

He shut his eyes and gulped.

This Sphinx would eat him all the way to the bone.

Wait!

That was it. Bone. That was the answer.

But did he want to live like this now?

He turned around to the other spacesuits. There were dusty, with skeletons inside, cleaned out bones. He turned back to her. "Sphinx?"

"Yes?"

"Has anyone ever found the answer to your riddle?"

"Not in time, no," she frowned.

"I see."

He looked up at the stars one more time. He liked the view, it was how he wanted to go. Looking up at the stars. He put his gloves back on, sealed them with the familiar hiss of pressurisation. He typed his responses one after another and held his finger over the button that would synthesise them all. With tears in his eyes, he pressed it.

His voice came out digitised and said. "Sphinxy, my answer is, water. My next answer is, flower. My next answer is, bullet. My next answer is, waterfall. My next answer is, rocket. My next answer is..."

It went on and on like that for a whole two minutes, reciting random things, whatever had come to his mind.

The Sphinx blew out her mist every time he gave a wrong answer, flaying another nanometre of his body.

When the voice synthesiser had nothing more to say, his spacesuit stopped moving completely, staying firm and upright from the automatics that helped him distribute the weight.

All that remained of him was the skeleton inside.

"And finally, my last guess," the synthesised voice said. "My answer is, bone. Choke on it, Sphinxy."

The Sphinx smiled and opened the gates behind her, then pushed the spacesuit through, letting it float into the void.

The End.

THE LAST STARGUNNER

"This plan sucks," the yellow alien said.

"No, can't you see? It's brilliant!" the green alien said, throwing his arms in the air. "Brilliant!"

"Okay, whatever. We're doomed anyway, might as well try this crazy scheme of yours," the yellow alien said, waving the issue away with his antennas. He looked down at the multidimensional screen. "Is everything in place?"

"The videogames? Yes. All set."

The yellow alien scratched his antennas. "How did you get them to download our game?"

The green alien snorted. "Oh, that was so easy. All we had to do was put up the words no-DLC on the cover image, and it got like a million downloads just like that," he said, clicking his fingers.

"Hm. And this race, you believe they're fierce warriors?" the yellow alien asked, pulling up the data of the human race. It was a weird kind of creature, bulky, primitive, with very small brains, hairy, no antennae. Not unless you counted the one dangling between his legs. So weird.

"Oh, they are the biggest gunners of the galaxy!" the green alien said proudly. He was right to be proud, he was the one who had discovered this race of brutes. If this long-shot worked, he'd be hailed a hero for all time. The yellow alien didn't thing this was their salvation, but on the off-chance it worked, he wanted to be on top of the project so he could grab all the praise.

"Do they kill?"

The green alien leaned close and whispered. "Without hesitation. Without mercy."

The yellow alien's skin prickled at that. Such a race! Killing with no remorse, it was inconceivable! But, weren't the Reds the same way? Invading their space, killing without mercy? Gunning everyone down, women, children, the elderly? Okay, the Reds were doing them a favour by ridding them of the elderly, but kids?

A travesty.

"I see..." the yellow alien said after a long moment.

"The battles have begun!" the green alien said, eyes wide as unidentified flying saucers.

The green looked down at the multidimensional screen again. It compressed a massive amount of information and beamed it to your brain, jumbling it all up, compressing it, then let your own brain sort it out. It was very efficient. The data coming in from the human servers was mind-blowing. The humans were killing each other relentlessly, all in a day's videogame.

The green's eyes went wide as well. "Don't they know?" he whispered, unable to take his eyes from the carnage.

"They do not seem to, no," the yellow said, gulping audibly.

"But... How is that possible?" the green witnessed a human team wiping out a team of 'noobs,' as they called them.

The other team respawned and regrouped, winning the next round. They called the opposing team, 'cyka blyat.'

It was impossible to look away.

"How can they not know?" the yellow alien cried out, blinking, still staring.

The green shook his head and wiggled his antennas in a shrug. "Perhaps their gods didn't tell them."

The yellow turned to his subordinate ally, shocked from top to bottom. "Didn't tell them the conditions for entry to the afterlife? How cruel can they be?"

The green wiggled his antennas in another shrug. "Very, it seems."

Twenty-four hours passed. The two allies took a few breaks but pretty much watched the entire slaughter. The humans were indeed the finest butchers in the galaxy. Here they were, killing each other without remorse. After he vomited a few times from his anus, the yellow alien managed to stomach the disgusting sight. He was tired, and his eyes were sleepy, but this was far too important to waste time on sleep. He shot up a stimulant and carried on, inspecting this crazy project.

"A winner has emerged!" the green alien cried out, kneeling on the floor of their spaceship.

The yellow alien felt the same, but he was a leader so he composed himself. The turned to look at the multidimensional information.

A teenager. Ianto Burkes. The best gunner in the entire planet.

"We've waited enough," the yellow alien said and pressed the button.

The teenager got snatched up by the teleport beam and found himself in the middle of the spaceship's bridge. He appeared there, shocked, his fingers still fiddling with imaginary controls. "Wha-"

The yellow alien stepped close to him. "We don't have time for shocked responses and debriefings." He booped the human's sticky forehead with his antenna and transferred everything he needed to know.

"Whoa!" the human said, eyes glazed. "Do that again."

"I'm afraid that would be a detriment to your health," the green alien said, rubbing his hands together. "Are you ready?"

"To kill the Reds? Hell yeah! Just point me at them," the human said, giddy for blood.

The two aliens turned to one another, the same thought clearly in both their minds. The same kind of hope. Could this kid be the one to save them from the Reds?

The yellow alien gave the order and a device where humans

played videogames on teleported in the middle of the bridge.

"Whoa!" the human said. This seemed to be his main reply to most things. But the yellow alien didn't care. He didn't bring the human here to talk. He brought him here to gun down his enemies.

"Are the controls known to you?" the green alien asked, worried.

"Yeah, man. Just like the retro games in my village. We can do this," the human said and grabbed the joystick of the arcade.

The aliens turned to each other, expectant, full of adrenaline. The yellow was weary, this could easily still be an elaborate plan to fool them. And if he fell for it, his entire race was gone.

The green alien nodded. "Control of the green armada, granted."

The yellow alien grunted. It was now or never. He flicked his antenna. "What the hell. Control of the yellow armada, granted."

"Whoa!" the human said, finding himself suddenly in control of two billion spaceships. "I know how to play this. How do I know how to play this?"

"We compressed the knowledge into the game. Never-mind," the green alien said. "Now, do it."

"Do what?" the human asked.

"Gun them all down. All the Reds," the green alien hissed, making a fist with his tiny fingers.

The human shrugged. "Sure."

And he turned to the arcade.

Both the yellow and the green alien retched and vomited the remainders of their stomachs. It was a complete massacre. The human simply outmaneuvered every single attack by the invading Reds, out-thinking them in every turn. His mind was, after all, alien to them. His actions made no sense, and by the time they regrouped the human called Ianto had wiped out significant portions of their fleet.

The yellow alien vomited from his anus, he didn't have anything left to expel, but his body convulsed in disgust.

"Eww, man!" the human said, turning away. "That's horrible. Why are you reacting like this?"

"How can you not know?" the yellow alien said.

"Know what, dude?"

"Your gods didn't tell you?" the green alien croaked, holding his stomach.

The bloodbath on the screen was unbearable.

"They don't tell us much of anything," the human Ianto snorted, killing Reds casually with tiny flicks of his wrist.

"The... How can I even begin to explain this... Every virtual sin, everything committed in all realities, is the same," the yellow tried to explain metaphysics to the dumb human.

Ianto kept gunning down enemy ships. "So?"

"Killing is a mortal sin! You'll go to hell!" the yellow alien wailed, unable to hold back. "Aren't you ashamed?"

Ianto shrugged. "It's just a videogame, dude."

The End

SPEAKING IN BUBBLES

It was hard, getting drowned the first time.

The second, not so much.

His implants acted like gills, filtering oxygen from the water and pumping it straight into his bloodstream. But he had to fight the instinct every time.

He had to drown, every time.

Willingly.

It was one of the few jobs Clytos could do. He wasn't qualified for anything. Grunts like him just had menial labour to do these days, and menial labour meant heavy body mods for tasks such as this.

He was building the new oil drilling platforms in the Aegean sea. The oil had been located decades ago, but instead of Greece actually drilling a hole for it and putting it to use, they waited till their loans defaulted and sold it off for peanuts to foreign interests. As in, corps.

So, a corp now owned the Aegean oil and was drilling for it.

Clytos drowned himself properly according to protocol. He had to make sure no bubbles were left in his lungs so that pressure was equalised and he could swim deep. When he did so, he grabbed the seadrone and it pulled him down into the blue darkness.

Once he got there, the seadrone projected instructions into his field of view. He was seeing normally in the water, all they had to do was add a layer over his eyes, like a permanent contact lens. It refocused light, or something like that, and he could see just fine, as long as there was light.

The drone shone at where the job was.

Clytos picked up a mechanical screwdriver from his tool-belt and started taking out rivets. One by one, the seadrone pointed out the next thing to do, the next tool to use, the exact movement and body positioning he should take.

He wasn't a very smart man. But he found himself wondering, if the seadrone knew so much about doing the job, why wasn't it doing it? It had a plasma torch like he did, it had manipulator arms, it had everything.

Nevermind. Clytos would be out of a job if that were the case, so he didn't want to look under that particular rock.

The Aegean sea was seismically active. So, when they brought the oil rigs out here and sank them in place, they sometimes went out of place. The sea floor literally shifted underneath them.

It wasn't something they couldn't fix, but it took some elbow grease.

Clytos spoke, breathing out water. The mic in his throat picked up his distorted voice. It was funny, he could say pretty much anything, but the sounds with the lips didn't work.

Aaa.

Ooo.

Mmm.

But he couldn't say 'b.'

So his report was, "Jo done. Whir to next?"

"Await instructions, Oceanid 3." The seadrone went silent after that.

So he waited. They must have done something to his body heat too. Oh, he wore a thick diver's suit, but he felt just fine, twenty metres down. He knew if he took his gloves off he'd lose all feeling in his fingers within minutes.

As he held himself on the oil rig handles, the undersea currents swept him around. He had gotten used to all the underwater effects. It was one thing that he was good at, being underwater. He knew that not all of the guys from his training went through with it, even after taking the mods.

He liked being alone down there, it was quiet.

As he moved with the current, he disturbed something. The rusted metal of the rig's leg lashed out and swam into his face. It touched him and it was sleek and wet, if you could call wet something that was already in water.

It was an octopus that had camouflaged itself, becoming one with the texture below. Now it was swimming around his head.

He knew that if he was a scuba diver like people used to do, he'd be very scared of the octopus right now. They tended to stick their suckers on the diving mask's glass, or tangle themselves in the air hose. Some scuba divers would panic and drown.

His father had lost a friend that way. So the warning was etched deep inside him.

But he needn't worry. So he played around with the octopus. He pushed it to one side and it let him manipulate it with the water wake. It became a sentient ball. Squishy and bouncy and tons of fun.

Now that the octopus had taken its normal, light brown colour, he could see it clearly.

He noticed that it had a stump. So it was a septapod.

"How should I nane you, little shurvivor?"

He played with it. It wrapped one leg around his fingers, then slid away. Clytos chased it and played some more. It had survived an attack, either a fisherman with a speargun or a bigger fish. He had lost a leg, but had lived to tell the tale.

"I'll call you Rusty. Yeah, that fits. Rusty."

Rusty swam around his head.

The seadrone whirred and caught up with him. "Oceanid 3, follow me for your next task assignment."

Clytos waved at Rusty. "Hafe to go to whork. Nye-nye."

The seadrone's side flashed and Clytos covered his eyes. When he looked again, the octopus was cut in half, burned and dead. The current swept Rusty away.

"Next assignment, Oceanid 3."

Clytos gripped his own plasma cutter. He turned his back to the seadrone and swam back to the rig. It's not like anyone could see his tears underwater.

The End

THE ROOT OF
THE PROBLEM

'Expose the root,' the instructions said. Okay, sure. But how?

Digger scratched his head and went through the file once again, scrolling without really focusing on any point in the ancient ypertext. The builders had created all these wonderful cyborg trees that give them all life, that give his entire village life.

Digger was an initiate, one of the few who had access to the sacred ypertexts and could read the code. The code of life, the code of the entire dome. For the dome gives life, and the dome takes it away.

Digger sighed and closed the holy tablet. It was running out of power for the day, and he needed to save some for tonight, if he was going to work through the night. That was the only way he'd make it in time, before the solstice. Why was the solstice such a problem?

Nobody actually knew. The initiates pretended to know, but they really didn't. Digger had asked all the questions in his mind, but he had gotten no real answer.

The problem was that the sacred ypertexts had been rewritten, censored through the ages, and Digger even suspected that they had added some bits to them to suit whatever law the initiates wanted to pass off as dogma.

Hundreds of little notes at the side of the ypertext, some even pointing to things that weren't there any more. That was a blatant clue that things were missing.

Really now.

Expose the root. Expose... the... Yeah, obviously, Digger said, rubbing his chin in front of the old tree. Its roots were exposed. How was he supposed to do it again? Or more? He unfolded his trusty shovel and started to dig around the cyborg tree, having nothing better to do.

After an hour or so he was hot and sweaty, left in his t-shirt. Digger sat back down on the dirt, then let himself fall on his back. He was one with the ground, one with the dirt, a holy communion.

Expose the root.

How, ypertext be damned? How was he supposed to do it? The ypertext seemed to consider this action such a normal step, it was the first one in every instruction. Nobody had ever seemed to crack it.

The hours were drawing near. He only had something like three hours until the solstice. That, the text said, would be bad if you hadn't 'run the S crypt.'

Another mystery. That S crypt.

Digger opened up his holy tablet, it wouldn't matter if the solar panels wouldn't recharge it, if his time was up, that was it. He scratched his head, rolled on the dirt between the exposed roots and tried once again for about the millionth time in his short life to decode the ypertexts.

He swiped angrily at random. "Bah! Nothing, nothing's in here..." he said, and threw the holy tablet to the side, making a puff of dirt whirl in circles.

He realised that this action was stupid, an initiate would never dishonour the sacred tablet like that. He picked it up again, mumbling a prayer for forgiveness. "Forgive me for my kernel is weak. Forgive me for I have sinned. Forgive me superuser."

He threw the holy tablet in his lap and focused ahead at the dim lights. His head leaned to the side, he was so tired. He was thirsty, and dirty, and frustrated beyond measure. All he wanted was a bath and some bread.

Digger idly swiped the holy tablet open, it was a gesture he did often with no particular reason. And his gaze fell on a word.

'Root.'

He stood up and gripped the holy tablet. Rubbing the sleep from his eyes, he quickly read the ypertext, scrolling up and down to go through every note there was. For the first time in his entire service, he had found a reference to the root!

Finally.

The ypertext said, 'To get to the root of the problem, go to the holy tree and open up a consul terminal.'

He knew how to do that! He quickly pressed the Ctrl, Alt and T buttons on the holy tablet.

The consul terminal's blackness showed up.

"Great! Now what?" Digger said to himself, going back to the instructions.

'Then enter su.'

That always baffled the initiates. 'Su' must have had a divine meaning, some said it was the short name for God. Digger was too tired to think theology, so he just took it literally.

He typed 'su' into the consul and pressed enter.

'When inside the roots, the hashtag should appear.'

Those hashtags were another point of contention amongst the initiate scholars. They said that it meant a lot to the ancients, for some arcane reason. They were obsessed with them, and with something else called emochi.

Anyway, there was no time. Digger scratched his head. Think, Digger, think. He had read some crazy guy's theory that the hashtags could also be represented as the symbol '#.' It always sounded stupid to Digger, but he was prepared to try anything. So, he checked the consul. And yes, there it was! The '#.'

By the Holy Tree, finally!

Okay, now what?

He read the rest of the instructions and followed them to the letter, reversing the translations by using his knowledge and utilising the ramblings of the crazy scholars. It turned out that the generations of initiates had somehow turned the holy ypertext into something that the holy tablet couldn't understand. But if you had spent years of reading all the research and the theories, you could follow the thread back to the original version of the ypertext.

Just how Linus Torvalds wrote it.

Digger typed in the commands, the trial-and-error took him more than two hours, but he was going at million-miles-per-hour now. He was typing and testing everything he could think of.

And as the last minutes counted down, and as the dome was ready to collapse, he finished it, following the instructions to the letter.

Digger pressed one final enter with a flourish and looked up. He felt woozy after such intense concentration, adrenaline leaving his body.

The Dome came to life.

Digger fell on his butt, clutching the holy tablet in his hands, looking up at the opening ceiling. It creaked and complained, but it opened up to the sky as the morning sun shone inside.

Digger could swear that he heard the cyborg tree sigh.

The End.

ASTROPITHECUS

Humanity went apeshit when the asteroid appeared in the sky. They called it the end of days, they called it Second Coming, they studied it from afar.

Humanity went even more apeshit when the asteroid appeared to be on a collision course with Earth. Men abandoned their wives, the poor looted from the rich, and employees told their bosses how they really felt about them.

Things only calmed down when the asteroid came and parked in a neat high-orbit around Earth. The world didn't end and there were a lot of awkward dinners for decades after that.

Naturally, they sent two astronauts up there to see what the asteroid really was. The first stepped outside, the second stayed on the shuttle for backup.

"Hey, Homo," was the last thing Alex Jones would expect to hear upon stepping foot on the asteroid. He must have imagined it, right? Just static, tricking his mind into thinking he could hear words that weren't there.

"Over here," the bass voice said again. Alex turned in his bulky spacesuit and looked around. It was still a vacuum, and the voice just came from his comms, so there was no real directionality. So, Alex just frantically looked around. He stopped when he saw the giant ape with a helmet on, waving at him.

"Hello. Can... You... Speak?" the giant ape mouthed the words as if he was speaking to a moron.

Alex gulped and shook himself back into action. All that recovery training from disorientation worked wonders right now.

He checked his oxygen levels, nope, he wasn't hallucinating due to an excess of oxygen. He blinked and decided to go for it. "Yes, I can hear you, loud and clear."

The giant ape seemed to relax. "Oh, good. I thought we'd have to draw things on the dirt or something. Welcome to my asteroid," he said invitingly, "I'm Rex, and you are?"

Alex took another minute to respond. "I'm Alex."

"Good… Thought I lost you again for a second there."

Alex clicked off his comms and left just the link to Earth, relayed from his ship. "Mission Control, do you have video?"

"Yes, Jones. Affirmative."

"Can you please describe what it is you're seeing on my feed?"

"Uh… A giant ape, basically. Over."

Alex cursed under his breath. He clicked his comm back to broadcast. "What are you?"

"Glad you asked!" Rex moved a bit closer and sat down, making Alex flinch. "I'm of the genus Astropithecus."

"Star… Ape? How do you know Greek?"

"How do you know Greek?"

"Nevermind that. Why did you call me gay when you first saw me?"

Rex seemed shocked. "I didn't!"

"Yes, you called me, 'homo.'"

"Yes, as in homo-sapiens, your genus."

Alex shook his head and scratched his helmet. If he had a wall around, he would bang his head on it. "Right, sorry. This is still a shock for me, you understand. First Contact and everything."

"What are you talking about, this isn't First Contact. This is an inspection," Rex the giant star-ape said casually.

"An inspection? Of what?"

"Of your uplift progress. You know, the next link in the uplift chain?" He shook his head. "None of this is ringing any bells, is it?"

"Absolutely nothing. Please explain."

"You know what uplift is?"

"Yes, the theoretical concept of gifting intelligence to a lesser species."

"Correct, but what do you call theoretical? This was your single task."

"I-I got nothing. Please take it from the beginning."

"We, astropitheci, uplifted you, homo-sapiens, to carry on and uplift the next species. You call them apes, I believe."

Alex shut his eyes, chewing on that new bit of information. "How are we going to do that?"

"If you haven't figured it out, then you're not ready yet! Inspection failed."

Alex cursed under his breath. Had he just done a blunder? A massive, hairy one? "And what are the consequences of that?"

Rex waved his massive hand away. "Ah, not much, we just call this a day, and I'll come back in fifty years, to the day, and check up on you."

"That's all?"

"That's all," Rex shrugged with his massive shoulders.

Alex's stomach went back to its proper place. Not dooming humanity by not offending an alien ape was a good thing to do for the day. "I'm sorry, but do you mind if I ask you some more questions? If they're inappropriate, please don't be offended, just tell me so."

"Sure."

"How are you exposed to space? Your body, I mean?"

Rex snorted. "We're called astropitheci, of course! Adapted to survive in space. I only need the helmet so that I have air to speak with you. I wouldn't expect you to know ASL."

"American Sign Language?"

"Astropithecus Sign Language, of course."

Alex pondered on it for a bit. No, he was a scientist. He couldn't accept it just like that. "I'm sorry, I don't believe you."

Rex looked offended. "About what?"

"That you can survive in a vacuum. That's impossible."

"What do you want me to do, take off my helmet?"

Alex said nothing, he simply mustered every last shred of bravado he had and tried to stare down the giant ape.

"Okay then," Rex said and took off his helmet. Air puffed away, and nothing else happened. Rex simply looked at him with his enormous, animalistic but intelligent eyes, and then scratched his nose in relief. Alex could see him mouthing something like, 'Oh, yeah, I needed this.'

"This is impossible," Alex muttered.

Rex made some hand gestures. Alex couldn't read them at that point, but analysts later deciphered them as, 'Do you believe me now, you hairless butt?'

Then he put the helmet back on, and the air cycled. "See?"

"I-I still can't believe it."

"Well, there it is. What else do you want to know?"

Alex braced himself for this question. This was a historic moment, everything was recorded and transmitted back to Earth. He chose his words carefully. "Do you claim that you are the ones who uplifted my species?"

"Yes," Rex said simply.

"And who uplifted you?"

"The Titans."

"Who are they?"

"Basically larger versions of you, about two times my height."

Alex shut his eyes for the tenth time in this mind-boggling mission. The amount of information was giving him a headache, and it wasn't just the booming voice of his conversation partner. "There are giant humans, twice your size, you say, and they gave you intelligence."

"Yes," Rex nodded.

"And where are they?"

"They left us like centuries ago."

"Oh. Sorry to hear that. And that is the uplift chain? They uplifted you, you uplifted us, and now you want us to uplift our apes back on the planet?" Alex pointed towards Earth. It was easy to do, she covered half the sky.

"Pretty much, yeah."

Alex breathed in deep. The stale air wasn't helping him feel better. "And the size difference, it's relevant somehow, right? You say the Titans look human, are twice your size, you are, well, ape-like, easily twice my size, maybe more, and then there's us. And the Earth-apes are smaller than us."

"You got it!"

"But, why?"

"No clue. It just is. And once you get to the next link in the uplift chain, they will uplift your short humans."

Alex was taken aback by that. "What do you mean? We don't have any short humans."

"Really? You should have them," Rex said, confused. Then he did something and the entire asteroid shook, the ground broke, Alex fell down on his knees.

An enormous machine emerged from the asteroid's ground.

Mission Control went insane. "Jones, report. We're seeing a weapon-like object emerging from the ground. Report, what is it?"

"I-uh… I don't know."

Rex turned his back and tinkered with something on the object. It looked like a cannon. Or, a telescope. Or, a cannon. Fuck!

"Jones, there are fourteen nuclear missiles primed and ready, report right this instant. Is it a weapon?"

Alex gulped. He couldn't be sure. What if it was? Rex was very intelligent, he could have been lying to him this entire time. "No, it's a telescope."

"Jones, please forget about your self-preservation right now, the entire world is at stake. Report! Is it a telescope or a weapon?"

Alex was sweating. He couldn't be sure, not really. This was an alien piece of machinery, made by frickin' space apes! How could he possibly know?

How could he possibly make the right decision?"

"Mission Control, abort the launch. It's a telescope. I repeat, abort, it's a telescope."

"Are you certain?"

Alex gulped. "Yes."

"Affirmative. Launch is aborted. Hope you're right…"

Alex couldn't breathe, he checked his levels. They were all right, it was all psychological. Rex turned to him, unperturbed by the commotion he caused. "See? There, I see them, short humans. Look."

Alex walked awkwardly in the tiny amount of gravity and looked in the telescope's display. "Yes, those are children."

"Exactly! Those are the ones your apes need to uplift. The short ones."

"No, I'm sorry, that doesn't make sense. Our children are the same genus as us. They grow up to be homo-sapiens, they are, homo-sapiens."

Rex tilted his massive head and squinted naughtily. "Are they?"

Alex thought about it. "Wait, you have to be talking about pre-pubescence. That's the only stage where we differ."

"Exactly! I knew you could figure it out."

"But still, that doesn't make them a different species."

Rex grunted. "Ungh, it kinda does. You don't really let them grow, you assimilate them. Children have different thinking, and they are sexless, non-hormonal people. It's only once they start producing oestrogen and testosterone that they start hitting each other and doing… other things."

Alex took a step back, and he was still trying to scratch his head over the helmet. "Wait, so we're gonna uplift our apes, and they will somehow uplift our offspring into the next stage of human evolution? Is that what you're saying?"

Rex gave him a wide smile. "I'm so glad they sent a clever one. This could have gone so badly."

"But, who started the Uplifts?"

Rex shrugged. "Probably someone really big." He opened his massive arms wide. "Like, reaaally big."

"And why the alteration between our species?"

"Oh, that I can answer. We're symbiotic, and we help each

other out. That's how it has been for millennia."

"Okay, no problem with that, I'm all for helping each other out. But why can't we ourselves uplift our short ones?"

"Because you're too close to the problem, can't you see? You can't work on yourselves without preconceptions, and neither can we. We both need the outside point-of-view from the other."

"Recapping here: only we can figure you guys out, and only you can figure us out. Genetically, evolutionally, etcetera."

"Yes, hairless one."

"Rex, my brain hurts."

"It's okay, I understand. I'd offer you some water but I don't know how to give it to you."

"It's okay, thanks anyway. I need to ask you some things, again, if they're somehow offensive, please just let me know."

"Sure."

"Are you considered, you know, big, for your species?"

Rex stood up and his bulk was impressive. "Yes, didn't my name give it away? I'm one of the bigger ones, if I may say so."

"Okay. Next question. Rex, why did you ride an asteroid to come visit us?"

Rex chuckled. "What was I supposed to ride, a tin can full of air and fuel?"

Alex glanced back at his own ship. He decided not to press that particular issue. "Hey, Rex, are you alone up here?"

"Nah, I brought my family along."

Alex perked up. "Really? Where are they?"

"I'm not bringing them up to see you, you're ugly, you'll scare the kids!"

"Okay…"

Rex laughed, rumbling the vicinity for a long while. "Nah, I'm messing with you. It's just me and Ben, the navigator."

"Oh. Can I meet him too?"

Mission Control butted in at that instant. "Jones, what are you doing? This is a security risk, you can't handle two astropitheci together. Over."

Alex clicked the broad comm off. "As if I can handle just one. He could have crushed me anytime. Over."

Rex carried on. "No, I'm not calling him up here. He's so boring. I swear, I'm doing you a favour."

"Fine then. What else? Oh, you said this isn't First Contact?"

"Pft, no! Haven't you seen the monuments by the Titans back on your planet? It's been millennia, but these guys put their faces on EVERYTHING. So megalomaniacal, they liked to play god with primitive yous."

Alex gulped. "Rex, please clarify for me, are you saying that the mythological depictions around the world of giant people are not metaphorical?"

"Nope."

Alex bit his lip, and wanted to chomp down till it bled. His mind was racing, but he couldn't bother with philosophy right now. This was a once-in-a-lifetime opportunity to gain information about the evolution man. Of man, alongside the ape.

Oh, man.

Rex clapped his hands together. It was weird, because Alex expected to hear a massive clap, but there was nothing in the vacuum of space. "Okay, since you're not ready for the inspection, there's no need for me to stay here any longer. One last question, and I'm off. After you take off in your little shuttle, of course. Unless you wanna join us. But, no, it's too soon."

Alex's heart now raced. One question. He knew he was gonna regret whatever decision he made for the rest of his life.

He needed something that would kick the stupid people back home into gear, something that would end the endless debates and inane discussions this meeting would spark.

Something... hopeful.

Biting his lip, he asked, "Rex, last question. I need to know if the only way for humans to survive the adversity of nature is by working along with your kind."

Rex gave him a massive, toothy smile. "Yes, Alex Jones of Earth, the only way forward is by working together."

"Thank you," Alex said, and turned to leave. Then he

stopped. "No, I need to recap. For my superiors, to make it clear what you want from us, avoid miscommunication. It's not a new question."

Rex chuckled. "Okay. Recap."

"You want us to figure out how to uplift our apes."

"Yes."

"And you want us to then work with them, to figure out how to uplift our own species."

"Correct."

"And you'll be coming back to inspect our progress in fifty years, to the day."

"Well, give or take a week, Alex. This is an asteroid, not a tree-vine. It drives like a small moon."

Alex snorted, looking around. "I guess it does. Rex, can I shake your hand?"

"Of course!" Rex shuffled his giant bulk forward and extended his hand.

Alex shook it, somehow. It was more of a gesture, but he thought it mattered.

"You have upended everything for us, you know that?"

Rex shrugged. "Same thing that happened to us from your ancestors. You'll be fine."

"Are you sure?"

"Definitely. Now go, you have so many things to figure out and not a lot of time to do so."

"Don't we have fifty years?"

"Fifty years is just an eye-blink."

The End

DID YOU ENJOY THESE STORIES?

Leave a review on the store you got this from or on Good-reads.

For more stories like these, join the Mythographers and get your free starting library in your email:

https://mythographystudios.com/join

www.ingramcontent.com/pod-product-compliance
Lightning Source LLC
Chambersburg PA
CBHW021403160726
47994CB00007B/3063